THE SPACE RACE
and Other Stories

Collins

Contents

Unit 4

Core: The Space Race 6

Challenge: How King Steve Defeated
　　　　　Duncan the Undefeatable 20

Unit 5

Core: What Made King Alfred So 'Great'? 34

Challenge: A Chance to Say Thank You 48

The Space Race

Written by Mio Debnam

How did a race between the USSR and the US to travel to the moon become such an important part of history?

Read on to understand some of the key events of the Space Race – a time when two enemies risked everything to dominate space.

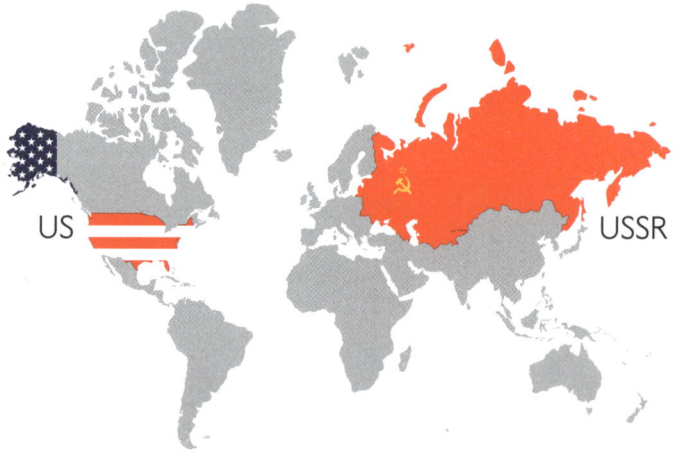

The USSR existed from 1922 to 1991. It was made up of 15 parts called republics.

1957

The USSR celebrated a major victory by sending Sputnik 1 into space. This spacecraft changed history, as no man-made object had orbited our planet until then.

It was a very risky flight – so risky that it didn't have any people on the spacecraft.

The team in the USSR was relieved when Sputnik 1 was able to orbit safely. But they still weren't sure if a living thing could withstand the dangers of space travel.

They hadn't even figured out how to bring the spacecraft back down!

Just weeks later, the USSR sent Sputnik 2 into orbit, carrying a stray dog called Laika. Laika demonstrated that living creatures can make it into space. But sadly, when in orbit, she didn't live for long.

1958

In response, the US sent Explorer 1 into space in 1958. Although it didn't carry any living things, it was a great achievement. But the USSR still had the edge in the race.

Later the same year, the US created an agency to study space and space travel: NASA. The race was heating up!

1959

In 1959, the USSR sent up a spacecraft that made history once again. It managed to escape our planet's gravity and reach the moon, but it didn't land on it.

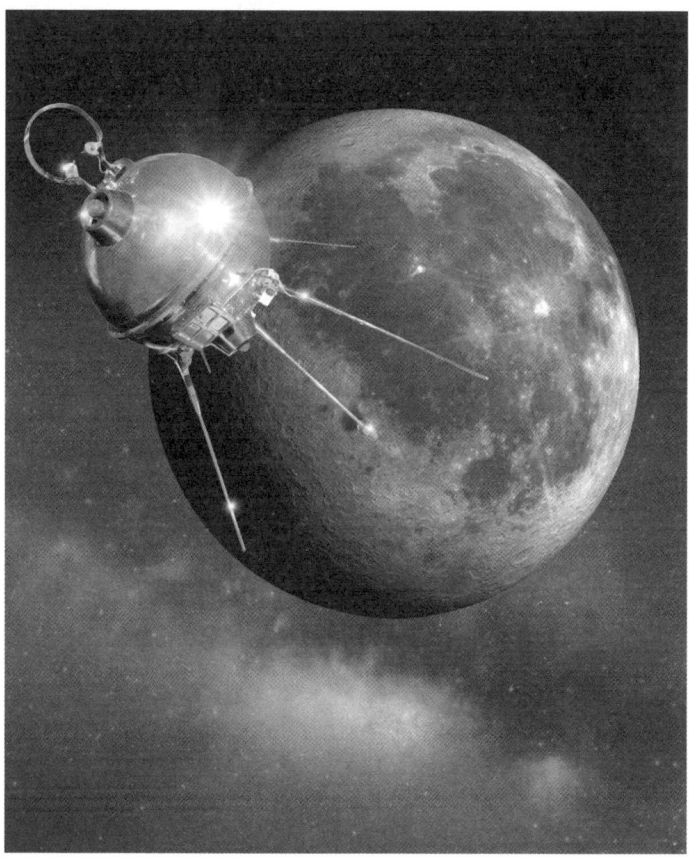

1961

In 1961, the USSR pulled off a magnificent feat by sending a person into space. A man called Gagarin orbited our planet for 108 minutes until he landed safely back in a field.

Three weeks later, the US sent a man called Shepard into space. His trip lasted just 15 minutes, and he didn't manage to orbit our planet.

The USSR was still in the lead.

1962–1967

Soon after, US President Kennedy made his famed speech. He said:

"We choose to go to the moon [...] not because it's easy, but because it's hard."

And it was. For the next six years, NASA faced many setbacks as they struggled to send their team to the moon.

1968

In December 1968, NASA celebrated a remarkable achievement. A spacecraft with three of their team members orbited the moon. No person had orbited the moon until then! The US was back in the race.

1969

NASA changed the game in 1969 when their next spacecraft landed on the moon. Neil Armstrong went down in history as he stepped onto the moon's surface. This was a major achievement for the US.

650 million people witnessed the moon landing on TV!

So, who was the winner?

It's hard to say who was the real 'winner' of the Space Race.

The USSR didn't put a person on the moon, but they did win the race to get a person into space.

The teams from the US and USSR each made a range of significant breakthroughs.

Maybe it can be said that the two were winners in different ways.

People in space now

At the start of the Space Race, everyone who went to space was male. But these days it is fairer and lots of women have travelled to space, too.

This SpaceX team is made up of people from three different continents.

No person from the UK had been to space until 1991, when Helen Sharman made history.

Jessica Watkins is the leading African American woman to be an ISS team member.

Wang Yaping exited her spacecraft and stepped foot in space to set up equipment!

How King Steve Defeated Duncan the Undefeatable

Written by Gareth P Jones

Illustrated by Michela Di Cecio

"Lords and ladies!" a voice rang out. "Please be upstanding for our freshly crowned leader ... King Steve the Brave!"

Everybody in the grand chamber clapped and whooped. "Duncan the Undefeatable is conquered," they chanted. "Long live King Steve!"

Steve beamed. "Yes, I have indeed achieved this victory single-handedly."

"A-hem," Sheena nudged Steve.

"And thanks to my remarkably brilliant partner, Sheena," Steve quickly added. "Now, please join me in this celebratory feast of greasy meat."

"Sorry, if I may, your majesty," said Lord Sneedy. "We would all like to hear how you defeated the undefeatable King."

"You don't really want to hear that story, do you?" said Steve.

"Yes we do!" everybody responded.

"Well then," began Steve. "I was born on a dark and dingy night. The wind was howling from the east – "

"Maybe speed it up a little, my dear," said Sheena.

"Fair point," said Steve. "As some of you will remember, I was a simple shepherd, tending to my sheep on Peachy Top Ridge – "

"*Our* sheep," Sheena interrupted.

"Sorry, yes. Anyway, I had a sudden but brilliant thought to turn these bleating creatures into lethal assassins. I spent a bit of time training the woolly killers. When they were all set, we demolished Duncan's army."

"In fact, Steve, it was *I* who trained the sheep," said Sheena. "And it took years, not just 'a bit of time'. And, yes, they helped us get through the outer defences of the palace, but that wasn't how the King was defeated, was it?"

"Ha, yes, that is right," said Steve. "For that, we needed the help of ... the Green Wizard."

Everybody gasped, for the Green Wizard was the greatest wizard in the land.

"It took me years to convince him to help us," said Steve, "but I did it for all of you."

Everybody clapped. Although many of the lords and ladies were enemies, they all agreed that Duncan the Undefeatable had behaved very badly indeed.

"Thank you, King Steve," said Lady Fudge. "Duncan was a mean and greedy king. We are grateful to you for your bravery."

"In reality, it was *I* who asked the Green Wizard," said Sheena. "I'd helped him escape from the Dungeon of Despair last year, so he was happy to assist in return."

"But the heat-seeking darts were down to me," said Steve.

"Oooo!" said the crowd.

"That's right. In general, darts just go straight through the air. But, at my request, the Green Wizard bewitched them to swerve, target and poison the beastly King."

"Duncan wasn't poisoned by one of your darts though, was he?" said Sheena.

"Do we have to go into this now, sweetie?" whispered Steve through gritted teeth.

"Maybe you should tell the real story," suggested Sheena.

"Yes, tell us the real story," agreed Prince Bilge.

"Well, what really happened is that I challenged the King to a game of chess," said Steve.

"Wow, you beat Duncan at chess?" said Chief Pete of the Heath-Dwellers.

"Er … " Steve glanced furtively at Sheena. "No. Duncan beat me," he admitted.

"Then how did you defeat him?" asked Lord Scissorly.

"I let Duncan win," said Steve, "then as he celebrated, I unsheathed my sabre and — "

"Dropped it on your feet," finished Sheena.

Everybody laughed.

"As Duncan was chuckling at my silly husband's foolishess, I knotted his shoelaces together," explained Sheena. "He got up, stumbled and accidentally fell into his palace's pit of doom."

Briefly, the chamber was still. You could hear a pin drop ...

... until a voice rang out, "Everybody, be upstanding for our real leader ... Queen Sheena the Brave!"

"Bother," sighed Steve, toasting the Queen.

Kingdom map

What Made King Alfred So 'Great'?

Written by Lindsay Galvin

Baby of the family

No English king or queen has been given the title 'Great' – except Alfred. So, what did this king achieve that made him so acclaimed?

Alfred was born in 849 to the King and Queen of Wessex, which was one of the Saxon kingdoms. He was unlikely to become King because he was the fifth male child.

A tiny victory

Alfred loved to study and read books. When he was a child, his mum set the family a challenge of memorising a book of rhymes. Alfred's teachers recited it to him, and he remembered it, beating all his bigger siblings in the task!

Raid to invade

Alfred's parents died by the time he was nine. Danish Vikings had been carrying out raids for Alfred's entire childhood, until they finally invaded England. The majority of the Saxon kingdoms were absorbed into a Viking land. Wessex was the one Saxon kingdom that was left.

Map of the Saxon kingdoms

Training for battle

In his teenage years, Alfred's love of studying became a side quest to his army training. When he was sixteen, Alfred was in active service, fighting the Vikings alongside his male siblings. But they did not win many battles.

King in combat

By the age of twenty-one, all of Alfred's male siblings had died, so he was crowned King of Wessex in April 871.

Alfred inherited a weakened kingdom that was under attack. Many powerful Wessex lords turned against him to join Guthrum, the Viking chief.

Feast to flight

In 878, Alfred was at a feast when Guthrum carried out a surprise attack. Alfred was forced to take flight and hide in the wild marshes of a village.

According to legend, a farmer's wife asked him to keep an eye on the cakes she was baking. Distracted by the problems in his kingdom, Alfred let her cakes burn. He accepted her telling off without admitting that he was, in fact, King!

Battle of Edington

Hiding in the marshes, Alfred was at rock bottom. But still, he didn't shy away from his responsibilities as King. He rallied forces and defeated Guthrum at the Battle of Edington. This was a significant victory, which demonstrated his strength as King.

Strategies for defence

Alfred needed ideas to turn the tide and defend his kingdom from the Vikings. With his quick mind, he came up with several strategies:

1 Building fortified settlements with ramparts topped with rubble or wooden fences, and bordered by ditches. These stopped Viking raids.

2 Organising a shift pattern for his fighters. This allowed part of his army to spend their time fighting to defend the kingdom, while part rested and tended to their farms.

3 Cutting off Viking supply lines to weaken them.

4 Building a fleet of battleships to defend the coast.

Peace time

At last, Alfred made peace with the Vikings.
He joined the Saxon kingdoms back together.
He finally had time to return to his childhood love
of reading and writing.

Alfred understood the importance of literacy
and wanted to improve skills in his kingdom.
He studied Latin and translated Latin texts into
English so that a greater number of people could
read them.

A great legacy

Alfred the Great died in 899 aged 50 or 51. By this time, he was accepted as King of all Saxons. He even had a coin with his face on!

He set the stage for his descendants to wipe out Viking dominance. With a quick mind and epic fighting, Alfred deserved to be called Great!

Alfred's battle tactics

Smart battle tactics were important for defence. These were two of Alfred's key strategies:

Strategy 1: Shield barricade

Fighters stood side by side in battle and locked shields. This prevented the enemy from getting through. When the shields were locked, the battle became a contest of pushing and trying to stop spears from thrusting through any gaps.

Strategy 2: Army shift cycle

Alfred split his army in two and they worked in different shifts.

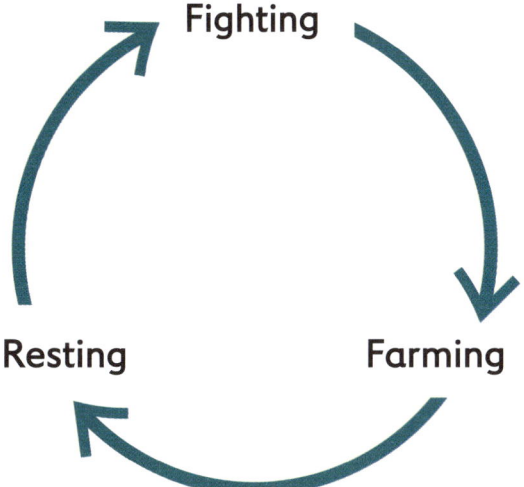

This model allowed for crops to thrive, which made sure there was enough food, while the kingdom was being defended. Plus, it helped to prevent fighters from getting too tired and burning out, as they had time to rest.

A Chance to Say Thank You

Written by Tony Bradman

Illustrated by Eduardo Rubio Rincón

My name is Layla, I am fifteen, and this is my story. I am writing this as a record, so that you who are not yet born will hear the history of our age ...

I lived with my family once, but then The Bad Time came. Wild storms wiped out the cities and colossal waves drowned the land.

The Bad Time was like a horror film. But I survived. I was saved by a relief boat and taken to a tiny island that had once been the top of a hill. I believed I was lucky to find dry land, but I soon realised I had come to an evil place.

The majority of the survivors were teenagers, and everything was run by The Committee of Elders. There were three Elders and they had a team of Protectors, who were a bunch of mean assistants. We were directed to work on the island's farm for very long, tiring shifts. But the Elders and the Protectors never seemed to help.

"Why are you complaining?" the Chief Elder said angrily one day, when a teenager cried out that they were tired and hungry. "You kids should be grateful – we Elders have to go without as well. We're all in this together."

Yet their faces were shiny and their bodies strong and wide, while we looked drained and fragile.

It didn't feel right, I thought.

Then something happened that changed everything.

I couldn't sleep one night. At last, I decided to stop trying and slipped out of the dilapidated barn where we were made to live. I crept through the muddy fields to The Big House. I made certain the Protectors didn't see me, then sneaked up and peeked in.

To begin with, I had no idea what I was looking at. The Elders were sitting at a long table, which was groaning with all sorts of plates, bottles and glasses. They were eating and drinking and laughing – then I realised that they were having a feast!

I hadn't seen so much food and drink in one place since The Bad Time had begun. It was then I realised that we were being exploited. The teenagers worked the fields all day long, and the Elders were laughing at us as they feasted on the food we farmed. I was horrified. It was incredibly unfair.

"Here's to simple-minded teenagers who don't challenge us!" said the Chief Elder, raising his glass. "And importantly, here's to keeping us Elders free from hunger."

Their greed and lies made me so angry! I wanted to burst in and yell at them. But I realised that wouldn't do any good. They would simply call for the Protectors to punish me for spying, and I didn't like the idea of that. Still, I had to do something ...

Then I had a brilliant idea.

The next morning, I reported back to everybody in the barn. They were just as angry and badly wanted to do something, too.

But they soon settled down when I revealed my plan. "We have to pick the right time to trick and defeat them –"

So, we spent our nights plotting and planning. We gathered all the string we had for farming and hid it. We behaved ourselves and never complained. We complied with every order the Elders gave us, however hard or mean or mindless.

Then one night we offered to put on a play for the Elders and the Protectors. "I'm sorry if we haven't seemed grateful," I said. "Think of this as a chance for us to say thank you."

"Excellent," said the Chief Elder, smiling. "We could do with a bit of fun."

But fun was the last thing on our minds. The Elders were full and sleepy from their large evening meal. So, we invited them into the barn. Once they were sitting, not suspecting anything ... we quickly tied up their arms and legs, like parcels!

Soon our triumph would be complete. Our final act was to push our enemies out to sea on a boat.

And from that day on, we lived much happier lives.

Then and now

I lived a happy life with my family prior to The Bad Time. Here we are, in the park on a sunny day.

It all changed when The Bad Time arrived. Terrifying floods swept everything away.

To begin with, life on the island was insufferable. We were so tired from working the fields all day, every day.

But we took a stand and took power. Now we make sure everything is fair.